The New Adventures of
MARY-KATE & ASHLEY ™

The Case Of The
SUMMER CAMP CAPER ™

Look for more great books in

series:

The Case Of The Great Elephant Escape™
The Case Of The Surfing Secret™

The Case Of The
SUMMER CAMP CAPER™

by Judy Katschke

■HarperEntertainment
A Division of HarperCollinsPublishers

A PARACHUTE PRESS BOOK

PARACHUTE
PRESS

DUALSTAR
PUBLICATIONS

Parachute Publishing, L.L.C.
156 Fifth Avenue
Suite 325
New York, NY 10010

Dualstar Publications
c/o Thorne and Company
1801 Century Park East
Los Angeles, CA 90067

≝HarperEntertainment
A Division of HarperCollins*Publishers*
10 East 53rd Street, New York, NY 10022-5299

For information, address HarperCollins Publishers,
10 East 53rd Street, New York, NY 10022-5299

ISBN: 0-06-106584-6

HarperCollins®, ≝®, and HarperEntertainment™ are trademarks of
HarperCollins Publishers Inc.

First printing: June 1999

Printed in the United States of America

Visit HarperEntertainment on the World Wide Web at
http://www.harpercollins.com

10 9 8 7 6 5

1

THE PRINCESS PALACE

"Where is everybody?" I asked my twin sister, Ashley.

Ashley plopped her duffel bag on the floor of bunk seven. She brushed her strawberry-blond hair out of her eyes. "That's no mystery, Mary-Kate. We're the first ones here."

It was the first week in July. Ashley and I usually spend our summers solving mysteries. We run the Olsen and Olsen Mystery Agency out of the attic of our house. But this summer our parents let us come to Camp Wishing Well—a really cool sleep-away camp. It was our second time at a camp, but our first time at Camp Wishing Well.

Ashley and I checked out the cabin. There were five bunk beds lined in a row. Between each bed was a small cubby shelf.

All of the beds were empty except for one. It was already made with pink sheets and a flowered quilt. There was even a little stuffed bear on the pillow.

"Hey, we're *not* the first ones here." I crossed my arms across my chest. "Looks like you jumped to a conclusion before you knew all the facts, Ashley."

"Oops." Ashley gave me a weak smile. "Good thing we're not trying to solve a mystery right now."

Ashley is always telling me to think things through when we solve mysteries, and to get all the facts before making a decision. *I'm* the one who usually jumps in with both feet.

"I guess there's a first time for everything," I told her.

We chose a bunk bed against the wall. It was right next to a big, sunny window.

"I get the top bed!" I called out. I tossed my duffel bag on the mattress. Then I glanced out the window. It faced the main path that led to the mess hall and the mail hut.

A parade of campers were heading toward their cabins. Some of them carried backpacks. Others dragged big, heavy trunks.

"I wonder where Tim's bunk is," I said.

Tim Park is one of our friends from home. It was his first time at sleepaway camp.

"I know how we can find him. Just look for a trail of candy wrappers and follow it!" Ashley joked.

I knew just what Ashley meant. Tim

loved food more than anything in the world.

"Do you think Princess Patty will be in our bunk?" Ashley asked as she laid some flowery sheets on her bed.

I giggled. "If she is, we'd better make room for all of her clothes!"

Princess Patty's real name is Patty O'Leary. She's our next-door neighbor. She usually gets everything she wants. And this time she'd wanted to go to Camp Wishing Well with us.

I started making my bed. My blue flannel sheets made me feel right at home. So did my favorite sweatshirt. I got it at the zoo on a class trip. It had a hood, a zipper, and the coolest zebra print.

Just then the screen door flew open. Two girls came into the cabin, dragging trunks. They looked nothing alike, but they were wearing identical plaid shorts and green T-shirts. The tags on their trunks told me their names—Jackie Higgins and Jody Raskin.

"Hi," Ashley said. "I'm Ashley Olsen."

"And I'm Mary-Kate Olsen," I added. "Welcome to bunk seven."

The girls didn't say a word. They stared at our bunk beds.

"What's wrong?" Ashley asked. She looked at her bed. "Is there a worm on my pillow or something?"

Jody and Jackie marched over to our beds. They began yanking off the sheets.

"Hey!" I shouted as Jody tugged at my flannel sheets.

Jackie grabbed Ashley's pillow.

"What are you doing?" Ashley shrieked.

"Cut it out, you two!" A girl with red hair and freckles ran into the cabin. She pulled Jody and Jackie away.

"Stay out of this, Marcy," Jody snapped.

"Yeah," Jackie said. "They took our beds!"

"What do you mean, *your* beds?" I asked.

Jody flipped her long blond hair over her shoulder. "We come to this camp every year," she said. "We always get the bunk beds by the big window."

"But the beds were empty when we came in," Ashley explained.

"And we didn't see your names on them," I said.

Jody and Jackie mumbled something to each other. They turned around and stomped to the other side of the cabin.

"Thanks for sticking up for us," I told Marcy. "I'm Mary-Kate and this is my twin sister, Ashley."

Marcy smiled. "Don't pay any attention to Jody and Jackie," she said in a low voice. "They're just two spoiled princesses."

The door flew open and Patty walked in. She dropped her matching suitcases on the floor. "What a dump!" She groaned.

"Speaking of princesses…" I whispered to Ashley.

"If I find one bug, I'm out of here!" Patty marched around the bunk. Instead of a T-shirt and shorts, she was wearing a dress splashed with huge sunflowers.

"The bathroom better have a huge mirror," Patty said as she went to check it out. "And big fluffy towels."

"Where does she think she is?" Jody asked Jackie. "In a fancy hotel?"

I was just about to unpack my clothes, when Patty let out a huge shriek. I ran to the bathroom door. "Are you okay, Patty?" I called.

"There's only a *shower* in here!" she said. "How am I going to get through four weeks without a strawberry bubble bath?"

Ashley and I rolled our eyes. How were *we* going to get through four weeks of living with Princess Patty?

"Oh, well," Patty said. She walked to the

big wooden closet along the wall. She opened it and grabbed some wire hangers. "At least I brought all my new summer clothes with me."

"You're not using all those hangers, are you?" Jody asked.

"Of course," Patty said. "Why?"

"What about our stuff?" Jody asked. "You can't hog all the hangers!"

"Besides," Jackie said, "we have more clothes than you do."

Patty looked Jody and Jackie up and down. "Maybe. But mine are nicer."

"Welcome to the Princess Palace," Ashley whispered to me.

Another girl came into the cabin. We introduced ourselves. The girl's name was Sophie. She seemed very nice. Then our counselor, Amy, stepped in.

"Hi, girls!" Amy said. "Welcome to Camp Wishing Well."

Amy looked about twenty years old. She

had shiny brown hair and sparkling brown eyes. Her T-shirt read CAMP WISHING WELL—HEAD COUNSELOR.

Sophie pointed to her T-shirt. "You're in charge of the *whole* camp?" she asked.

"That's right," Amy replied. "But I still like to hang out with the campers. So I'm going to be your counselor, too!" Amy looked around the bunk and counted heads. "We seem to be missing one camper."

The door opened. A girl with curly dark hair came inside.

"You must be Veronica," Amy said.

"Hi," Veronica said. She walked straight to the bed with the teddy bear on the pillow. Then she froze. "Hey! I left a bag of cookies on my bed. Now they're gone!"

We all gathered around Veronica.

"Maybe they fell under the bed," Amy suggested.

Veronica looked under the bed. When

she stood up, she was holding an empty cookie bag.

"The bag is here—but the cookies are gone!" Veronica cried. "I had six cookies left. Someone ate them!"

"That's too bad, Veronica," Ashley said.

I saw Jackie and Jody whispering to each other. After a few seconds, they walked over to Veronica.

"We know who stole your cookies, Veronica," Jody said.

"Who?" Veronica asked.

"The only people who were in the bunk when we came in," Jackie said. She turned around and pointed at me and Ashley. "Them!"

A PILLOW FULL OF
CANDY WRAPPERS

"**M**ary-Kate, Ashley?" Amy asked. "Is that true? Did you take Veronica's cookies?"

"No way!" I said, shaking my head.

"You tell 'em, Mary-Kate!" Tim's voice called out.

I turned. Tim was standing in the doorway next to a boy with blond hair and glasses. The boy was munching on a rice cake.

"Oh, no. Boys!" Jackie yelled.

"Our bunk is being raided!" Jody shouted.

"And it's only the first day of camp!"

"That's just our friend Tim," Ashley told Jody.

Tim pointed to the blond boy. "And this is my new friend, Clark Mitchell."

Clark raised his rice cake. "Hey."

"We were walking past your bunk. We heard everything." Tim turned to Veronica. "You probably ate your cookies and forgot. I always forget what I eat."

Patty groaned. "Who can keep track of what *you* eat, Tim?"

"You shouldn't be eating cookies anyway," Clark told Veronica. "They aren't good for you."

Veronica wrinkled her nose. "What?"

"I snack on rice cakes, baked peas, and an occasional prune roll-up," Clark said. "My parents don't let me eat cookies. They're junk food."

"Who cares?" Jody snapped. She pointed to me and Ashley. "We have thieves in our bunk. Sneaky, horrible thieves!"

"Thieves?" I said.

"Us?" Ashley cried.

Amy turned to Jackie and Jody. "Girls, you shouldn't go around blaming your bunkmates. They said they didn't do it."

"Besides," Tim said, "Ashley and Mary-Kate Olsen aren't thieves. They're the Trenchcoat Twins."

Marcy's mouth fell open. "You mean the famous detectives?" she asked. "I read all about you in a magazine."

"They've been solving mysteries since they were little kids," Tim bragged.

"Our great-grandma Olive is a detective," I explained. "She taught us everything we know."

Tim turned to me and my sister. "Clark and I are in bunk nine," he said. "That's on the main path, too."

"Great," I said. "Thanks, Tim."

The boys walked to the door. Clark

glanced over his shoulder. "If you don't find your cookies, Veronica, try cauliflower chips. They're delicious."

"Cauliflower chips?" Veronica gagged. "Yuck!"

Tim and Clark left the bunk.

Amy put her arm around Veronica's shoulders. "Your cookies might still turn up," Amy said. "In the meantime, let's not jump to any conclusions."

"That's what Great-grandma Olive always says." I nudged my sister. "Right, Ashley?"

"That's right," she said.

Amy left the cabin. Ashley and I continued to unpack. I could see Jackie and Jody glaring at us as they made their beds.

"Wow," Ashley whispered to me as she rolled socks. "Our first day of camp and we're accused of a crime."

"I know." I groaned. "What a welcome!"

*   *   *

"Way to go, Mary-Kate!" Ashley cried. "You hit a grand slam!"

I rounded the bases as fast as I could. My teammates cheered when I slid into home plate.

It was late Tuesday morning—the third day of camp. Bunk seven had just won a close softball game against bunk six.

"I can't believe you scored six runs," Marcy told me as we left the softball field.

"I believe it," Jody said. "If anyone knows how to *steal* bases, it's Mary-Kate Olsen."

Then Jody and Jackie started to sing: "Who stole the cookies from the cookie jar? The twins stole the cookies from the cookie jar…"

When Jody and Jackie were ahead of us I turned to Marcy. "Are those two always so creepy?" I asked.

Marcy nodded. "For as long as I can remember."

"Attention all campers," a voice said over the camp's loudspeaker. "The first care packages of the summer arrived this morning. They will be handed out at the mail hut in exactly ten minutes. Be there or be square."

A cheer rose through the camp. Care packages meant goodies from home!

"Let's go!" Patty called. "My parents are supposed to send me something from Paris!"

Ashley and I followed the other campers and Amy to the mail hut. It was a white cabin with an American flag hanging over the door. A huge crowd of kids stood in front.

I saw Tim heading our way. "Hi, Mary-Kate. Hi, Ashley." Tim's fingers were tightly crossed. "Are you guys feeling lucky?"

I nodded. "It would be nice to get a package from home."

"Nice?" Tim cried. "I've been dreaming

about my first care package for three whole days."

"But you brought a trunk full of candy, potato chips, and dip to camp," Ashley said.

"But that was only for the first day!" Tim exclaimed.

"Your friend Clark isn't here," I said, looking around.

"Can you blame him?" Tim asked. "Would you line up for a care package of cauliflower chips and alfalfa sprouts?"

All eyes were on the mail hut. The door to the hut opened. A teenage boy stepped out. He was holding a metal clipboard.

"That's Brett Valentine, the mail counselor," Tim said.

Brett looked up from his clipboard. "I have five care packages today."

"Please, please, please," Tim whispered.

Brett ran his finger down the clipboard. "They are for Sara Berger, Patty O'Leary, Mark Nehra, Angela Gonzalez, and Tim

Park." Then he went back into the hut.

"My care package is here!" Patty cried happily.

Tim jumped up and down. "Mine, too!"

Ashley and I waited to see what Tim and Patty got. When Brett came out of the mail hut again, he was shaking his head.

"Sorry. There are only four packages now," he announced. "One of them has disappeared."

"Disappeared?" Patty gasped.

Something wasn't right. How could a whole care package just disappear into thin air?

"Which one is gone, Brett?" Tim asked.

"Angela Gonzalez's package," Brett said.

"Thank goodness." Patty sighed.

A girl wearing a red T-shirt and tan shorts ran over to Brett. "What do you mean, my package disappeared? My mom wrote that she was sending me a whole box of chocolate Gooey Chewies and rainbow lollipops. And it was an overnight express package, too."

"Bummer," Brett said. But he didn't sound very sincere.

Angela walked away sadly. Then Tim and Patty ran inside to pick up their packages.

I shook my head. "For a mail counselor, Brett doesn't seem to care very much about the care packages," I told Ashley.

Amy took us all back to our bunk. It was letter-writing time. When we got inside, everyone started talking about the missing care package.

"I'm glad it wasn't mine," Patty said. She held up her hand. A bracelet dangled from her wrist. "My parents just sent me a gold bracelet with real diamonds. It's from Paris!"

"I'd rather have Gooey Chewies," Jackie muttered.

Patty stuck out her tongue at Jackie.

Then she climbed up on her bed. "And I'd rather rest than write letters. All these sports are wearing me out!"

But after a few seconds, Patty started tossing and turning. "Oooh!" she muttered.

"What's the matter, Patty?" I asked.

"These camp pillows are as flat as pancakes," Patty said. "At home I have two big, fluffy pillows—with ruffles!"

Jody sneered. "Maybe your mom can send you some from *Paris*."

Jackie put on a pair of radio headphones. "Quit complaining, Patty."

Patty sat up on her bed and pouted. "I need *two* pillows."

I sighed. "Here, Patty, you can use mine for now."

I reached for my pillow. But as I handed it over to Patty, something weird happened.

A shower of Gooey Chewy and lollipop wrappers fluttered out of my pillowcase!

WHO FRAMED MARY-KATE?

"Hey!" I shouted as the wrappers fell to the floor. "How did those get in there?"

Amy and my bunkmates stood around the heap of colorful papers.

"As if you didn't know," Jackie said.

"What do you mean?" I asked.

Jody pointed to the wrappers. "Gooey Chewies...rainbow lollipops. *You* stole Angela's care package, Mary-Kate."

"What's the matter?" Veronica sneered. "Weren't my cookies enough?"

"And why did you have to steal?" Patty asked. "I would have bought you some cookies if you wanted them that badly."

I didn't know what to say.

"Okay, girls, now let's give Mary-Kate a chance to explain," Amy said.

"But Mary-Kate would never steal anything," Ashley declared. "She doesn't even like Gooey Chewies. Right, Mary-Kate?"

I nodded. "They stick to my teeth."

"Then how did the candy wrappers get into your pillowcase?" Amy asked me.

"I don't have a clue," I told her.

Amy stared at the papers. Then at me. "I'm not going to make any judgments right now. But this doesn't look very good, Mary-Kate," she said.

"I know," I answered sadly.

Amy and the girls returned to their beds. While they wrote letters, Ashley climbed up to the top bed. She had her special notebook in her hand. The one she used to take notes about our cases. I used a tape recorder. It was in my duffel under Ashley's bed.

"What's that for?" I asked.

"I think you're being framed, Mary-Kate," she whispered. "Someone wants everybody to believe that you're stealing the goodies."

"But who?" I asked. "And why?"

Ashley leaned closer. "That's what we have to find out."

"I know," I replied. "This is serious. I wish Clue were here."

Clue is our basset hound. She helps us solve mysteries. She can sniff out clues from miles away. But we couldn't take her to camp with us.

We sat on my bed and thought.

"Maybe the real thief wants everyone to think I'm stealing the goodies so that no one will suspect him or her," I said after a while.

"I can see how someone could have

sneaked into our bunk to take Veronica's cookies," Ashley said. "But how could someone steal a care package right out of the mail hut? Especially if Brett was there all morning."

I snapped my fingers. "Maybe that's it," I said. "Maybe *Brett* stole the package."

"Hmm. He didn't seem to care when it was missing," Ashley said.

"Brett's the thief. Let's tell Amy," I said. I started to climb down from the top bed.

Ashley grabbed my arm. "Wait, Mary-Kate," she said. "Brett is a good suspect, but we shouldn't—"

"Jump to conclusions." I sighed. "I know. I know. I guess things are back to normal again, huh?"

"The Olsen and Olsen Mystery Agency is open for business," Ashley whispered.

"Open for business," I repeated, and shook my sister's hand.

* * *

After the letter-writing period was over, we put on our bathing suits and headed for the lake. Ashley carried her favorite striped towel. I could feel the stones under my flip-flops as we walked down the path.

Amy caught up to us. "Mary-Kate," she said. "I hope you know that I'll have to keep an eye on you from now on."

"But I didn't steal anything," I said. "Honest."

"I'd love to believe you, Mary-Kate," Amy replied. "But as head counselor, I have to consider all possibilities."

Amy walked on ahead of us. From the corner of my eye I saw Jackie and Jody give each other a high five.

"Great," I said. "Even my own counselor thinks I'm a thief."

Just then I heard a bunch of boys shouting and yelling. The noise was coming from Tim's bunk.

We all raced down the path toward bunk

nine. Tim and his bunkmates were standing outside.

"What happened?" I asked Tim.

Tim shook his head. "A jumbo can of cashew nuts was stolen out of Billy Singh's cubby."

"Here we go again!" Jody said, looking at me with narrowed eyes.

Ashley pulled me aside. "Let's check this out."

She pointed to a boy with dark hair. He looked upset.

"Is that Billy?" she asked Tim.

"That's him," Tim said. "Poor guy."

Ashley and I walked over to Billy.

"My sister and I are detectives," Ashley said. "Do you want to tell us what happened?"

"I brought the nuts from home," Billy explained. "I had the can in my cubby since the first day. I didn't even get to open it. Now it's gone."

"Did you see anyone suspicious near your bunk recently?" I asked.

Billy nodded. "This morning after breakfast I saw someone running out of the bunk."

"What did he look like?" Ashley asked.

"Like a zebra," Billy said.

The kids began to laugh.

"I know we have raccoons and skunks," Amy said. "But I've never seen a zebra at Camp Wishing Well!"

Patty put her hands on her hips. "Wait a minute," she said. "Mary-Kate is always wearing that tacky zebra sweatshirt."

I felt my blood freeze.

"So." Jody sneered. "Mary-Kate has a zebra sweatshirt."

"What a coincidence," Jackie said.

Tim waved his arms in the air. "Maybe a zebra escaped from the zoo. A zebra who loves cashew nuts!"

But no one seemed to listen to Tim.

Everyone was staring at me. The boys. The girls. Even Amy.

"Why doesn't anyone believe me?" I cried. "I did not steal the cookies, the candy, or the nuts. I am not a crook!"

"Don't worry. I know it's not your fault," Patty said.

"You mean it?" I asked her. Wow! Patty wasn't usually so nice to me. But now she really seemed to believe me.

Then she said, "Sure. My mom says that some people who steal can't help it. You have a problem, Mary-Kate."

I sighed. That was more like the old Patty!

"This is the second time a theft has been blamed on you," Amy said quietly. "Why, Mary-Kate?"

"I—I don't know, Amy," I replied. "Just give me a chance to figure it out. Okay?"

Amy bit her lip. Finally she nodded. "Okay, Mary-Kate." Then she walked away.

As the kids walked on, Tim put a hand on my shoulder. "I believe you, Mary-Kate," he said.

I lowered my head. "Thanks, Tim."

Tim went back inside his cabin.

"Ashley, let's go back to our bunk right now," I said. "I want to see if my zebra sweatshirt is still in my cubby."

"Good idea," Ashley said. "Maybe the thief stole your sweatshirt so everyone would think it was you."

We ran back to bunk seven. Since everyone was at the lake, the bunk was totally empty.

"Where do you keep your sweatshirt?" Ashley asked me.

"On my bottom shelf," I answered. I ran straight to my cubby and peeked in. Then I gasped. "Ashley!"

"What?" Ashley asked.

"My zebra sweatshirt," I said. "It really *is* missing!"

"Are you sure?" Ashley said.

"Where else would it be?" I asked.

"Try your laundry bag," Ashley suggested. "Maybe you stuck it in there and forgot about it."

I didn't remember putting my sweatshirt in my laundry bag, but I looked anyway. The sweatshirt wasn't in there, but something else was.

"Ashley!" I cried again. "Look what I found!"

4

NUTS!

"What did you find?" Ashley asked. "Is it your zebra sweatshirt?"

I shook my head. I reached into my laundry bag and pulled out a jumbo can of cashew nuts.

Ashley gasped. "Are those Billy's missing cashews?"

"I guess," I said, staring at the can. "Unless some squirrel is stashing food away for the winter."

My hands shook as I held the can. Amy

and the kids already suspected me. What would they think now?

"You're lucky you found the nuts when no one else was in the bunk," Ashley told me. "If Amy saw them, you would be thrown out of camp for sure."

"I can't be thrown out of camp," I said. "I didn't do anything wrong."

Ashley looked me straight in the eye. "That's why we have to solve this mystery as soon as we can."

I nodded. Ashley was right. I was not a thief—and I was determined to prove it!

"Come on, Ashley. Take out your note-book," I told her. Then I found my tape recorder. "Let's get working."

Ashley sat on her bed and started taking notes. I clicked on my tape recorder.

"Brett is our number one suspect," she said. "He had a chance to steal the care package. And since our bunk and Tim's bunk are on the way to the mail hut, he could have sneaked into both of them."

"What about Jackie and Jody?" I asked. "Remember when they gave each other a high five today?"

"They're still angry about us getting their favorite bunk beds," Ashley added. "Maybe they're trying to get back at us."

"Jody and Jackie are definitely suspects," I said.

Ashley jumped up. "Mary-Kate! I just thought of something. The robber is probably eating loads of candy. Do you know what that means?"

I shrugged. "He probably has loads of cavities?"

Ashley shook her head. "No. Mom is always telling us that candy will spoil our appetites, right?"

I nodded. "So the thief is probably so stuffed that he or she can't eat the food in the mess hall."

"When we go to the mess hall for lunch,

let's check out who's not eating," Ashley suggested.

I heard the sound of rustling leaves outside the bunk. Ashley must have heard it, too. She turned around.

"Quick!" Ashley whispered. "Hide the nuts!"

I glanced around for a safe hiding spot. "I'll put them back in my laundry bag," I said. "No one is going to go in there."

Ashley held her nose. "That's for sure!"

The sound turned out to be only a baby raccoon, but we left the bunk anyway. We didn't want Amy and our bunkmates to wonder why we weren't at the lake.

When we reached the shore, we put our towels on the grass next to Sophie. She had her camera with her.

"Aren't you going swimming, Sophie?" Ashley asked.

"No," Sophie said. "I don't want to leave my camera alone."

"I'll watch it for you," I offered.

Sophie looked at me strangely. Then she grabbed her camera. "No, thank you," she said quickly. She jumped up and ran over to Marcy.

"Oh, no." I sighed. It seemed as though everyone at camp suspected me. We had to solve this mystery fast!

At lunch in the mess hall, Ashley and I watched to see how much everyone was eating. Jody and Jackie were sitting at the end of our table. They gobbled down their tuna sandwiches. Patty had finished her sandwich and was staring into her plastic cup.

"We told you a zillion times, Patty," Jody snapped. "There are no bugs in the juice!"

"Then why do they call it bug juice?" Patty demanded.

I turned to Ashley. "Everyone is hungry here," I said in a low voice. Then I looked across the aisle to Tim's table. Tim popped the last crumb of his sandwich into his mouth.

But where was his friend Clark? I glanced around the mess hall.

"Ashley," I said. "I don't think Clark is at lunch."

Ashley stretched her neck to see. "I can't find him anywhere."

"Right," I said, excited. "And remember, Clark wasn't at the mail hut when Brett gave out the care packages."

"I think we have a third suspect," Ashley said.

I nodded. "Clark Mitchell."

After we finished our chocolate nut cake for dessert, Paul, the music counselor, got up to speak.

"There'll be a sing-along and marshmallow roast this Friday night at seven." He grinned. "That is...if no one steals the marshmallows!"

The whole mess hall began to laugh. I could feel my face flush as half of the kids stared right at me.

Paul sat down and Amy gave everyone the signal to leave. Tim caught up with us as we filed out of the mess hall.

Then I spotted Clark rushing past the mess hall. He pushed through a crowd of campers.

"What's his hurry?" I asked Tim.

"And how come he wasn't at lunch?" Ashley added.

Tim shrugged. "He was in the mess hall earlier. But he took one bite of his dessert. Then he said he had to leave."

Ashley and I glanced at each other. Clark was up to something!

"Come on, you guys," I said. "Let's follow him!"

5

CAUGHT SNOOPING

"Why do you want to follow Clark?" Tim asked.

"We'll explain as we go," Ashley said.

Ashley, Tim, and I ran after Clark.

He was racing up the main path. As we tried to catch up, I told Tim about my sweatshirt, the nuts—everything.

"You mean Clark is a suspect?" Tim asked. "But he's a great guy. He always gives me his lunch."

Ashley nodded. "And now we know why.

He's not hungry after eating all that candy!"

We tried to catch up with Clark, but he was way ahead. In a few seconds he was out of sight.

"Where did he go?" I asked.

"Let's check out my bunk," Tim said.

We ran up the path to bunk nine and peeked in the window. The cabin was empty.

"If Clark stole my zebra sweatshirt," I said, "I'll bet it's somewhere inside the bunk."

"Right. Let's search his cubby," Ashley suggested.

"Whoa!" Tim cried. "If the guys find out I let girls in our bunk, they'll put itching powder in my underwear!"

"You can be our lookout, Tim," I said. "Stand outside the cabin and make sure no one is coming."

"I don't know." Tim looked worried. "What should I do if I see someone?"

"Give us some kind of signal," Ashley said.

"Like what?" Tim asked.

Ashley shrugged. "Yell out, 'It's a beautiful day.'"

"But it's cloudy!" Tim declared.

"Just do it," I said.

"Okay, okay." Tim grabbed a handful of gummy fish from his pocket. "Clark's cubby is the one with the giant rubber eyeball on it. It was his science fair project in school."

"Yuck-o!" Ashley said.

The screen door to bunk nine creaked when I pulled it open. Ashley and I walked inside. The beds looked like they were never made. There were socks and under-shirts on the floor. A football poster was stuck to the wall with bubble gum.

"What a mess," Ashley said.

"It's a boys' bunk," I replied. "What did you expect?"

We found the cubby with the rubber eyeball on it. "Quick," I told my sister. "You look on the bottom shelves. I'll look on the top."

We pulled out Clark's clothes one by one. I glanced up at the rubber eyeball. I felt as if it were watching me.

"I can't find it," Ashley said.

"Then let's go," I said. "The boys will be here soon." I started to put Clark's things back.

The screen door slammed open.

Ashley and I whirled around.

Standing at the door was our counselor, Amy. She looked really angry.

"Mary-Kate? Ashley?" she demanded. "What are you doing in here?"

THE THIEF
STRIKES AGAIN!

"**U**h-oh," I muttered to Ashley. "We're caught."

Clark dashed into the cabin. "What's going on, Amy?" He looked at Ashley and me. "Hey! Were Mary-Kate and Ashley stealing my things?"

Tim opened the screen door and slipped into the bunk.

"Why didn't you give us the signal, Tim?" Ashley whispered.

"Sorry, guys. My mouth was full," he

said, chewing on a bunch of gummy fish.

Amy folded her arms across her chest. "Jody and Jackie told me they saw you sneaking into the boys' bunk," she said.

I rolled my eyes. Jody and Jackie—it figured!

"It's not what you think, Amy," I said.

"We weren't stealing anything," Ashley said. "We were looking for clues."

"So we could find the real thief," I added.

"Then why were you looking in *my* cubby?" Clark asked.

"We're looking everywhere," Ashley said.

Amy put a hand on Clark's shoulder. "Well, Clark can't possibly be the candy thief," she said.

"Why not?" I asked.

"Because a can of nuts was stolen today," Amy said. "And Clark is allergic to nuts, right?"

"Yup!" Clark said with a smile.

"I didn't know you were allergic to nuts," Tim said.

"I'm *very* allergic to them. That's why I had to leave lunch today," Clark explained. "I took a bite of cake, but I didn't know it was chocolate *nut* cake. So I had to go to the nurse."

That explains it, I thought. But I still had one question. "Where were you when Brett was handing out the care packages?" I asked Clark.

"In the nurse's office," Clark said.

"Again?" Ashley asked.

"I'm allergic to grass, too," Clark said. "And pine trees, and most types of leaves. Just about anything green."

"Clark is supposed to get his allergy shot every day," Amy said. "Right after the first activity."

My stomach felt as if it were twisted in knots. Clark was no longer a suspect—but I still was!

"Does that mean I'm clean?" Clark asked with a grin. "Like you detectives say?"

"You're clean," Ashley muttered. "But your bunk's a mess."

We followed Amy out of bunk nine.

"Good luck," Tim whispered to me.

"Thanks," I said. But I wasn't feeling very lucky.

When we were outside, I turned to Amy. "I didn't steal anything," I said. "You've got to believe me."

"I'd like to, Mary-Kate," she said. "Especially since I think you and Ashley are really good kids."

Ashley smiled. "You do?"

"Does that mean I can stay?" I asked.

"I'll hold off for now." Amy sighed. "But one wrong move and you're out. Is that understood?"

Ashley and I nodded slowly.

"Good," Amy said. "Now, why don't you girls hurry to the ceramics hut. It's time for arts and crafts. I'll see you later."

Our bunkmates were already in the ceramics hut.

"Hi, guys," I said.

All the girls stared at me and clutched their ceramic whales.

"Hold on to your masterpieces," Jody said.

"Yeah," Jackie giggled. "Sticky-Fingers Olsen might steal them, too!"

"Sticky-Fingers Olsen?" I cried.

"Just ignore them, Mary-Kate," Ashley whispered. "We'll get to the bottom of this soon."

Ashley and I took two empty seats at the long table. We sat next to Patty.

"Mary-Kate, Ashley." Patty held up her wrist. She pulled back the sleeve of her denim jacket. "Did I tell you that my bracelet has real diamonds?"

Jackie groaned. "About a zillion times."

I smiled at Patty. I was surprised that

she was still being nice to me, when every-one else thought I was a thief. But it made me feel better.

"It's a pretty bracelet, Patty. I wish I had one just like it," I said.

Zack, the art counselor, came over. "You'd better put the bracelet away for now, Patty," he suggested. "You might get paint on it."

"You're right," Patty said. She slipped off the bracelet and dropped it in her jacket pocket. Then she took off her jacket and hung it on the back of her chair. "I don't know what I'd do if I ruined my pure gold bracelet with real diamonds."

I tried not to think about the case as I worked on my ceramic whale. I painted the outside blue and the inside of his mouth bright pink.

"I hope we get to paint angels next," Ashley said.

"If I'm here that long," I mumbled.

"Let's clean up," Zack said when arts and crafts was over.

Ashley and Patty went to the sink to wash their brushes.

I stayed behind and painted big green eyes on my ceramic whale. Then I cleaned my brush and carried my whale to the shelf marked BUNK SEVEN.

Suddenly Patty let out a big scream.

"What's wrong, Patty?" Zack asked.

Patty was shaking her denim jacket upside down.

"My diamond bracelet!" Patty cried. "It's gone!"

7

GOING HOME?

"**G**ee, whiz," Jody said in a snippy voice. "I wonder *who* could have *stolen* Patty's bracelet." She stared at me.

"Well, it wasn't Mary-Kate!" Ashley snapped back.

"I'll bet it was," Veronica said.

Patty glared at me. "You said you wanted a bracelet just like mine!" she declared.

I tried to speak. The only thing that came out of my mouth was a little gasp. I couldn't believe this was happening to me!

"Come on, girls," Jody said. "Let's frisk her."

Jackie and Jody starting coming toward me. My voice came back just in time.

"Keep your hands off me!" I yelled.

"Girls! Girls!" Zack shouted. "A missing bracelet is serious business. I want you to go back to your bunk and wait for Amy. This is a matter for the head counselor."

Jody and Jackie glared at me as they huffed out of the ceramics hut.

"I still believe you, Mary-Kate," Marcy said quietly.

"Thanks, Marcy," I said. "Besides Ashley, you're the only one in the bunk."

Ashley and I walked slowly back to our bunk.

"We have to check out Jody and Jackie," Ashley said. "They're still suspects."

I nodded. "And don't forget about Br—"

"Hello, girls!" a voice interrupted.

Ashley and I turned around.

"Brett!" we said at the same time.

Brett handed over a stack of letters. "I got some mail for your bunk. Can you bring it over there?"

I didn't want Brett to know that we suspected him. I tried to act as if nothing was wrong.

"Sure," I said, taking the mail. "I hope Ashley and I got some mail from home."

"From what I've heard, Mary-Kate," Brett said, "it looks like you'll be going there soon."

I looked up from the letters. "Huh?"

"You know what I mean." Brett snickered. Then he walked away.

"Why is he so creepy?" I asked my sister.

"Maybe he knows we suspect him," Ashley said.

I checked through the letters. Then I noticed something strange. There were tiny brown smudges on all the envelopes.

"Look, Ashley." I pointed to a postcard.

"They look like fingerprints."

Ashley took a whiff of a postcard. "*Chocolate* fingerprints."

"You know what that means," I said. "Brett must be eating chocolate while he sorts his mail."

Ashley nodded. "Brett didn't just hand us the mail—he handed us a great clue!"

"Let's go check out the mail hut," I said.

"Mary-Kate, Ashley," Amy called from our cabin. "You're supposed to be in the bunk."

"We'll go to the mail hut later," Ashley said.

When Ashley and I walked into the bunk, Patty was sitting on her bed and sobbing. "My bracelet was from Paris," she cried.

I placed the mail on the bunk dresser. I knew Patty felt awful, but so did I. Whenever I felt sad at home, I'd snuggle up in my zebra sweatshirt. But since my sweatshirt was gone, I reached for my comfy sneakers instead.

Kicking off my sandals, I slipped my right foot inside. "Ouch!"

"What is it, Mary-Kate?" Ashley asked, sitting on her bed.

"There's something inside my sneaker." I pulled it off and shook it upside down.

CLINK!

Something gold and shiny fell out. Everyone gasped.

Patty jumped down from her bed. "That's my bracelet!"

"I know," I said. "But what is it doing inside my sneaker?"

Jody came out of the bathroom. "Oh, don't act so innocent, Mary-Kate," she said.

"You stole Patty's bracelet in arts and crafts," Jackie said. "And then you stuffed it inside your sneaker. It's as simple as that."

"How could you do this, Mary-Kate?"

Patty demanded. "I've known you for years and years."

"But I didn't steal your bracelet, Patty. I didn't!" I insisted.

Patty turned her back to me. "My mom says we should feel sorry for people like you, Mary-Kate. But I don't. I think you should go to jail!"

"But why would I dump your bracelet out of my shoe in front of everybody?" I asked.

"Maybe it was an accident," Sophie piped up. "Maybe you didn't mean for it to fall out of your shoe."

"No way!" Ashley jumped up. "Don't you see?" she asked. "Mary-Kate is being framed!"

"Quit covering for your sister," Jackie said. "Nobody believes her anyway."

I glanced at our counselor. Amy was staring at Patty's bracelet and frowning.

Then I turned to Marcy. "You believe me,

don't you, Marcy?" I asked.

"I believed you before." Marcy shrugged. "But Patty's right. You did say you wanted a bracelet just like hers."

Now *everyone* in the bunk thought I was a thief!

"Mary-Kate," Amy said. "I'm sorry—but I'm afraid I'll have to call your parents tomorrow morning."

"Why?" I gasped.

Amy sighed. "So they can come and take you home."

8

Spying For Clues

"If you go home, I'm going home, too," Ashley said during dinner that night.

"But you didn't do anything wrong," I told her.

"Neither did you," Ashley said. Then she smiled. "Besides, we're twins. We stick together no matter what."

I looked down at my macaroni and cheese. I couldn't eat a thing, and it was turning kind of crusty.

"I don't get it, Mary-Kate," Ashley said.

"If the thief has been stealing candy, why would he or she steal a bracelet?"

I shrugged. "Maybe it doesn't matter what's stolen," I said. "As long as *I'm* being blamed."

Ashley took a bite of her roll. "Well, don't start packing yet, Mary-Kate. We still have a whole night to solve this case."

Suddenly a paper airplane landed on my plate. I glanced up. My bunkmates were busy looking at a fan magazine.

"Where did this come from?" I asked Ashley.

"Unfold it," Ashley said. "Maybe it's a note."

I carefully opened up the airplane. A message was written in blue crayon: DON'T GIVE UP, MARY-KATE! YOUR FRIEND, TIM.

I glanced up and saw Tim smiling at me. He gave me a thumbs-up sign.

I gave him one back. The message made me feel a little better—but I still couldn't stop worrying. How were we going to solve this mystery?

After dessert, Amy stood up and made an announcement.

"There will be a game of bug bingo right here in the mess hall tonight," she said. "For those of you who don't want to play, there will be a movie in the recreation room."

"What movie?" a boy from bunk three called out.

"One of my favorites." Amy smiled. *"Willy Wonka and the Chocolate Factory."*

"Uh-oh," Jackie said. "If I were Willy, I'd put a lock on that factory."

"How come?" Sophie asked.

"Because Mary-Kate Olsen is here!" Jody answered.

As my bunkmates laughed, I wanted to disappear. Camp was turning into one big nightmare!

*   *   *

"You mean you're not going to the movie?" Tim asked us later that night.

The campers were heading toward the evening activities. It was getting dark. Everyone was carrying flashlights.

"Tim, the last thing I want to see is a movie about candy," I said. "Besides, we only have tonight to solve the case."

"And we haven't checked out the mail hut yet," Ashley said.

We told Tim all about the chocolate-stained envelopes.

"Come to think of it," Tim said, "my mail had chocolate fingerprints on it, too. But I thought they were mine."

"How are we going to snoop around the mail hut with Brett there?" I asked.

"Maybe he's not in the mail hut tonight," Ashley replied.

"I know," Tim said. "The counselors' schedule is always hanging outside the laundry hut. Let's check it out."

We took a pebbly path to the laundry hut. Sure enough, a schedule was hanging on a bulletin board. I read all the names until I found Brett's.

"Perfect!" I said. "Brett is working at bug bingo tonight."

"The coast is clear," Tim said. "Let's go for it!"

Ashley, Tim, and I ran to the main path. When we reached the mail hut, we peeked through the windows. It was dark inside.

Ashley pulled at the door handle. It swung open. "What luck!" she cried.

"Don't turn on the light," I suggested. "We'll use our flashlights instead."

"Wow," Tim said. "Now I really feel like a spy!"

I shone my flashlight around the room. Brett's desk was against one wall. On the other wall was a shelf filled with cardboard boxes.

Ashley stood on a stool and checked out

the boxes. I aimed the light at them.

"Are they care packages?" I asked.

"No," Ashley said. "They're filled with supplies."

I searched all over Brett's desk. I could hear Tim opening the file cabinets in the back.

"Any clues?" I asked.

Tim and Ashley shook their heads.

Tim's eyes suddenly grew wide. "Wait!" he cried. "There's candy around here. I know it!"

"How?" Ashley asked.

Tim tapped his nose. "I can sniff out sweets anywhere!"

"But we looked all over," I said.

Just then I heard a noise. It sounded like talking.

"Did you hear that?" I asked my sister.

Ashley nodded. "Sounds like it's coming from the back."

I searched the back of the mail hut.

There was a narrow door next to the file cabinets.

Ashley pressed her ear against the door. "There's definitely somebody back there," she whispered.

"Who?" Tim asked.

I put my hand on the doorknob. "There's only one way to find out."

I held my breath as I opened the door a crack.

We peeked inside—and gasped.

Inside the small room was Brett. He was surrounded by a crowd of seven-year-old boys from bunk four. They had chocolate-smudged faces and hands.

"Okay, guys," Brett said. "How many of you like Gooey Chewies?"

The boys raised their grubby hands. They began jumping up and down. "Me! Me! Me!" they cried.

I looked closer. There was a table filled with envelopes. It was also filled with chocolate, caramels, and lollipops!

"Mary-Kate," Ashley whispered. "Look at all that candy."

"I told you my nose never lies," Tim whispered.

"Just as I thought," I said in a low voice. "Brett Valentine is the thief."

"Let's get him," Tim whispered. He leaned forward—and knocked the flashlight out of my hand. It fell down with a loud *clunk!*

I held my breath as the boys glanced at us.

"Look, Brett!" a boy with glasses shouted. "Spies!"

9

A JUMBO CAN OF CLUES

Spies? They thought we were spies?

There was only one way to handle this. Ashley and I marched into the room with Tim right behind us.

"Where did all this candy come from?" I demanded.

"None of your beeswax!" Brett growled.

"And why aren't you at bug bingo?" Ashley asked.

"What for?" Brett asked. "All I had to do was set up the chairs. My job is done."

A tough-looking kid with stick-on tattoos tugged at Brett's sleeve. He held out his hand.

"Come on, Brett," he said. "I just sorted a gazillion postcards. Pay up!"

"Okay, okay," Brett said. He reached into the bag and handed the boy a chocolate Gooey Chewy.

Then I figured it out. "You're paying these kids with candy to sort your mail, aren't you?"

"So that explains the chocolate finger-prints." Tim glared at Brett. "Pretty sneaky, Brett."

"Look." Brett sighed. "Sorting the mail is a big drag. I'd rather hang out with my buddies, if you must know."

"It's not the mail we want to know about," I told Brett. "It's all that candy."

Tim folded his arms. "Is it from stolen care packages?"

"No way," Brett said. He looked hurt. "I

may be lazy, but I'm not a thief."

"Then where did all that candy come from?" Ashley asked.

"I buy it in town every week," Brett replied.

"He sneaks out." The boy with the tattoo smirked.

"Shut your trap, Haggerty," Brett warned.

"How do we know you're telling the truth?" I asked.

Brett reached into his pocket and pulled out a piece of paper. "Read it and weep."

I glanced at the paper. It was a receipt from the Big Onion Supermarket. "Two bags of Fruity Froggies, three bags of rainbow lollipops, and four bags of Gooey Chewies."

"Mmm." Tim licked his lips.

"Now do you believe me?" Brett asked.

Ashley and I nodded slowly.

"Can you guys please leave us alone

now, so we can collect our candy?" a spiky-haired boy said.

"You mean, you *like* doing Brett's work?" I asked the boy.

"The work is boring," he replied. "But the pay is awesome."

"I'll say!" Tim smiled at Brett. "If you need any more help…"

I grabbed Tim's arm. "Come on, Tim. Let's go."

We left the mail hut. It was dark, so we had to use our flashlights. The air was chilly and I missed my sweatshirt.

"Brett was our last suspect." Ashley sighed.

Our feet made crunching sounds as we stepped over twigs and dried leaves. An owl hooted from a tree.

"I guess I should start packing," I said slowly.

"Mary-Kate," Ashley said. "I told you a million times. You are *not* leaving." She shone the flashlight in her face so I could see how serious she was. "Remember what Great-grandma Olive always says? Clues always turn up when you least expect them."

"And the Trenchcoat Twins never give up," Tim added.

"You're right." I gave them both a high five. "We'll solve this case if it takes us all night."

"You bet," Tim said. "There's just one little thing."

"What?" Ashley and I asked at the same time.

"Seeing all that candy in the mail hut made me hungry," Tim said. "I can't solve a crime on an empty stomach."

"Since when is your stomach ever empty?" I asked Tim.

"Do you still have those nuts in your laundry bag, Mary-Kate?" Tim asked. "I could really go for some cashews."

"You want to eat our evidence?" Ashley cried.

"Just one or two—or maybe three," Tim begged. "Pleeeease?"

"Okay, okay," I said. "I guess one or two couldn't hurt."

Tim followed Ashley and me into bunk seven. Everyone was either at the movie or at bug bingo.

I opened my laundry bag and pulled out the big can of nuts. Then I popped off the plastic lid. "We're going to need a can opener," I said. "This can was never opened."

Tim shrugged. "I guess the thief doesn't like nuts."

I looked up from the can. "Or maybe," I said slowly, "the thief was *allergic* to nuts. Guys, this time I really think I know who the thief is!"

"Who?" Ashley asked, her eyes wide.

"Clark Mitchell!" I answered.

"But I thought you ruled out Clark," Tim

said. "How can he still be a suspect?"

"The person who framed me always left wrappers and empty bags," I said. "That means he or she ate whatever was stolen."

I held up the can of nuts. "This can is sealed," I explained. "That means the thief never touched the nuts. Maybe because the person is allergic to them."

"Like Clark!" Ashley said, smiling.

I dropped the evidence back into my laundry bag.

"Are you going to tell Amy about Clark?" Tim asked.

Ashley shook her head. "We can't prove that he did it."

"We don't have much time," I said. "We have to find Clark and follow him everywhere he goes!"

Suddenly I heard a twig snap. I glanced up at the window and saw a flash of black and white.

My heart began to pound. I knew that

black-and-white print anywhere. It was my zebra sweatshirt!

"Come on, you guys!" I cried, jumping up. "We've got a thief to catch!"

Two Mysteries Solved!

Ashley, Tim, and I dashed out of the bunk. I shone my flashlight along the path. A figure was running away in the distance.

"It looks like a boy," Ashley said quickly. "And he's carrying some kind of bag."

"Stop!" I shouted.

The kid glanced back at us. The zebra-striped hood covered most of his face. He started running faster.

Ashley, Tim, and I chased the boy up the main path. We ran past the mess hall.

"He's too fast!" Tim puffed.

"Come on," Ashley cried. "We can't lose him!"

We were racing toward the rec room, when the thief stumbled.

"Oof!" he grunted, and fell to the ground.

"Grab him!" I shouted.

The boy lay facedown on the path. He was surrounded by crushed potato chips.

"Thought you could get away from us, huh?" Tim grabbed the boy by the shoulder and flipped him over.

Ashley and I both gasped.

"It *is* Clark!" Ashley said.

"And my sweatshirt!" I said.

"And my barbecue chips!" Tim cried.

Clark opened his mouth wide. Then he screamed, "Help! Help! The candy thieves are stealing my potato chips!"

The door to the rec room swung open. Amy and the campers ran outside. They gathered around us.

"What's going on out here?" Amy said.

Clark was about to say something, when Patty stepped forward.

"Hey. That's Mary-Kate's sweatshirt," Patty said. "I'd know that tacky—I mean—*zebra* sweatshirt anywhere."

Clark stood up. He dropped the bag on the floor and brushed away some greasy crumbs.

"Clark?" Amy asked. "Do you have something to say?"

We waited for Clark to speak. It was so quiet, you could hear the crickets chirping.

"Okay, okay," Clark finally said. "You caught me. I'm the candy thief."

"Yes!" I pumped my fist in the air.

"But, Clark," Amy said. "Your parents don't allow you to eat junk food."

"That's the whole point!" Clark cried. "I can't stand all that healthy food they make me eat. I only pretend to like it. But all I can think about is junk food!"

Tim sighed. "I know the feeling, pal."

"No, you don't, Tim," Clark said. "*You* can eat candy anywhere. If *I* want to eat it, I have to do it secretly. Even in my own house."

"Your house?" Amy asked.

Clark nodded sadly. "I stash cookies in my shoe bag. Lollipops inside my books. I even hide jawbreakers inside my gym sneakers."

"Gross," Ashley muttered.

I almost felt sorry for Clark. But then I remembered how he framed me.

"You got all the candy you wanted," I said. "So why did you have to get me in trouble?"

"I'm sorry, Mary-Kate," Clark said. "When I found out your bunkmates thought you stole Veronica's cookies, I got the idea to frame you. Then no one would suspect me of being the thief. It was perfect!"

"But why did you steal the nuts if you

couldn't eat them?" Ashley asked.

"That was just to throw everyone off," Clark said. "I guess it worked for a while."

"Wait a minute," Amy said. "How did you take the care package from the mail hut? You were with the nurse getting your allergy shot."

Clark lowered his head. "I snuck into the mail hut before I went to the nurse. Brett wasn't around, and so—"

"So you stole my care package!" Angela cried.

"And my cashews," Billy said.

"And my cookies!" Veronica yelled.

"Thief! Thief! Thief!" the campers began to chant.

Amy held up her hands. "Okay, everybody. Calm down." She turned to Clark. "I understand why you stole the snacks, Clark," Amy said. "But why would you steal Patty's bracelet? I don't get it."

Clark looked confused. "What bracelet?"

he asked. "I never stole any bracelet. Honest!"

"You lied all this time about the candy," Amy said. "Why should we believe you now?"

Clark stared down at his sneakers.

Amy turned to me. "I'm sorry for not believing you, Mary-Kate. You were telling the truth all along."

"Does that mean she can stay in camp?" Ashley asked.

"You bet she can," Amy said with a grin.

Ashley and I gave each other a big hug.

"Yahoo!" Tim cheered.

I glanced over at my bunkmates. Sophie, Marcy, and Veronica were smiling. But Jody and Jackie looked angry.

"As for you, Clark," Amy said. "I'm calling your parents right now. Will you come with me to the main office?"

Clark gulped. Then he his face turned a weird shade of green. "Can we go to the

infirmary instead?" he asked.

"The infirmary?" Amy asked. "Why?"

Clark grabbed his stomach. "All that candy...I think I'm going to...be sick!"

"Oh, no!" I cried. "Not on my zebra sweatshirt!"

As Clark's counselor rushed him to the infirmary, Veronica walked over to us. "I'm sorry I blamed you for my cookies, Mary-Kate," she said.

"Thanks to the Trenchcoat Twins, there'll be no more missing goodies from now on," Sophie said.

"Wait!" Patty cried. "We still don't know who stole my bracelet. And it's worth thousands and thousands of dollars!"

"Give me a break," Jody grumbled. "It probably cost three dollars and fifty cents."

"Yeah," Jackie muttered. "It made our wrists turn green."

"How do *you* know?" Patty demanded. "I never let you try it on."

I stared at Patty. She was right. How *did* Jody and Jackie know? Unless...

"Jackie? Jody?" I said. "You're the ones who took Patty's bracelet, aren't you?"

Jody turned to Jackie. "You had to open your big mouth, didn't you?"

"But it was your idea!" Jackie cried. "You're the one who picked up Patty's bracelet when it fell out of her jacket. We hid it in Mary-Kate's sneaker so the twins would get sent home. So we'd get our old bunk beds back."

"I can't believe it! What a sneaky thing to do!" Ashley said.

"Big deal," Jody said. "This is camp, not school. We can do whatever we want."

"Oh, really? Well, now you'll be doing it at home," Amy said. "I'm calling both your parents, right now."

Jody and Jackie looked horrified. They ran after Amy as she walked toward the main office.

"You can't send us home, Amy!" Jody pleaded.

"My ceramic whale isn't dry yet!" Jackie cried.

"Wow," Patty said. "I'm sure glad those two are going home."

"Because they stole your bracelet?" Ashley asked Patty.

"And tried to get me in trouble?" I added.

"No," Patty said. "So I can get their closet space. And their cubby shelves, and their shower pails, and…"

Ashley and I looked at each other and smiled. The case of the candy thief was finally closed. From now on it would be four whole weeks of fun.

And that made us very happy campers!

Hi from the both of us,

Ashley and I were on vacation at an awesome resort! There was a big hotel, a beautiful beach, and lots of kids our age. We were even taking surfing lessons so we could enter the big surfing contest.

The competition was fierce. Even Scott, our surfing instructor, was "hanging ten" against us! The best surfer of all was a girl named Tiffany. We thought she was sure to win—until someone tried to frighten her out of the competition!

First her new surfboard was painted pink. Then she got threatening notes. And that was only the beginning! You'll never guess who was behind all the pranks. It's a whale of a mystery!

Have we got you hooked? Turn the page for a sneak peak at our newest adventure: *The Case Of The Surfing Secret.*

See you next time! *Love,*

Ashley Olsen + *Mary-Kate Olsen*

The Case Of The
Surfing Secret

Tiffany's dad looked at his watch. "Is your class starting soon?" he asked. "I managed to slip away from my meeting for a while. But I've got another important meeting in half an hour."

"But I'll be here for the rest of your lesson," her mom told her.

Sometimes companies hold big meetings at hotels. *Tiffany's dad must be an important businessman,* I thought.

Tiffany's parents unfolded a blanket and sat down to watch.

"Okay, guys," Scott called out. "Let's try some of this stuff out in the water."

I dragged my surfboard closer to the

ocean. Then I stuck my toe in the water. It was cool—perfect for a hot day.

Ashley kicked some sea foam at me. "It looks like the time you put too much soap powder in the washing machine!"

We waded out till the water reached our waists. Then we hopped on our boards and paddled out.

For the first time, I actually felt nervous. Was it because of the waves? They were definitely the biggest I'd seen so far this trip. Or maybe it was that scary note.

T.J. paddled up beside us. He started singing some scary music—the kind of music they always play in movies when a shark is about to attack.

"Stop!" I said, laughing. "You're giving me the creeps!"

"Shark!" Ashley screamed.

Yeah, right. "Ha, ha, Ashley," I said. "Very funny."

But Ashley wasn't laughing.

And then I saw it.

A shark fin was slicing through the water.

Heading straight for me!

No. Wait. I'm wrong, I thought.

I stared as the gray fin moved through the water.

The shark wasn't swimming toward *me* at all.

It was headed straight for Tiffany!

"Tiffany!" I cried. "Look out!"

"Swim!" Ashley screamed.

High Above Hollywood Mary-Kate & Ashley Are Playing Matchmakers!

Check Them Out in Their Coolest New Movie

Mary-Kate Olsen

Ashley Olsen

Billboard DAD

One's a surfer. The other's a high diver. When these two team up to find a new love for their single Dad by taking out a personals ad on a billboard in the heart of Hollywood, it's a fun-loving, eye-catching California adventure gone wild!

Now on Video!

DUALSTAR VIDEO

The Adventures of MARY-KATE & ASHLEY™

Look for the best-selling detective home video episodes.

The Case Of The Volcano Adventure™
The Case Of The U.S. Navy Mystery™
The Case Of The Hotel Who•Done•It™
The Case Of The Shark Encounter™
The Case Of The U.S. Space Camp® Mission™
The Case Of The Fun House Mystery™
The Case Of The Christmas Caper™
The Case Of The Sea World® Adventure™
The Case Of The Mystery Cruise™
The Case Of The Logical i Ranch™
The Case Of Thorn Mansion™

YOU'RE INVITED TO MARY-KATE & ASHLEY'S™

Join the fun!

You're Invited To Mary-Kate & Ashley's™ Costume Party™ *NEW*
You're Invited To Mary-Kate & Ashley's™ Mall Party™ *NEW*
You're Invited To Mary-Kate & Ashley's™ Camp Out Party™
You're Invited To Mary-Kate & Ashley's™ Ballet Party™
You're Invited To Mary-Kate & Ashley's™ Birthday Party™
You're Invited To Mary-Kate & Ashley's™ Christmas Party™
You're Invited To Mary-Kate & Ashley's™ Sleepover Party™
You're Invited To Mary-Kate & Ashley's™ Hawaiian Beach Party™

And also available:

Mary-Kate and Ashley Olsen: Our Music Video™
Mary-Kate and Ashley Olsen: Our First Video™

DUALSTAR VIDEO

Two Times the Fun!
Two Times the Excitement!
Two Times the Adventure!

Check Out All Eight *You're Invited* Video Titles...

... And All Four Feature-Length Movies!

And Look for Mary-Kate & Ashley's Adventure Video Series.

Listen To Us!

Ballet Party™

Birthday Party™

Sleepover Party™

Mary-Kate & Ashley's Cassettes and CDs
Available Now Wherever Music is Sold

It doesn't matter if you live around the corner...
or around the world....
If you are a fan of Mary-Kate and Ashley Olsen,
you should be a member of

Mary-Kate + Ashley's Fun Club™

Here's what you get
Our Funzine™
An autographed color photo
Two black and white individual photos
A full sized color poster
An official Fun Club™ membership card
A Fun Club™ School folder
Two special Fun Club™ surprises
Fun Club™ Collectible Catalog
Plus a Fun Club™ box to keep everything in.

To join Mary-Kate + Ashley's Fun Club™, fill out the form below
and send it along with

U.S. Residents	$17.00
Canadian Residents	$22.00 (US Funds only)
International Residents	$27.00 (US Funds only)

Mary-Kate + Ashley's Fun Club™
859 Hollywood Way, Suite 275
Burbank, CA 91505

Name:_____

Address:_____

City:_____ St:_____ Zip:_____

Phone: (_____) _____

E-Mail:_____

Check us out on the web at
www.marykateandashley.com